The Noisiest Class Goes to the Beach

Pauline Hill

illustrations by Joan Beales

HIPPO

Hippo Books
Scholastic Book Services Inc.
London

Scholastic Book Services Inc.,
10 Earlham Street, London WC2H 9LN

Scholastic Inc.,
730 Broadway, New York, NY 10003, USA

Scholastic Tab Publications Ltd.,
123 Newkirk Road, Richmond Hill,
Ontario L4C 3G5, Canada

Ashton Scholastic Ltd., 165 Marua Road,
Panmure, Auckland, New Zealand

First published by Scholastic Book Services Inc., London, 1985.

Text copyright © Pauline Hill, 1985
Illustrations copyright © Joan Beales, 1985

ISBN 0 590 70332 3

All rights reserved
Made and Printed in Hong Kong by Everbest Printing Co., Ltd.
Typeset in Plantin by Keyline Graphics, London

In summer
It's very hot in our school.
Even in our swimming pool
It's not cool.

Our classroom is very hot.
We loll in chairs. Who cares?
Too hot to read. Too hot to make a noise.
"What's wrong with you?" our teacher, Miss Baker,
wants to know.
"Why are you so quiet? You're not like my class at all!
My class is THE NOISIEST CLASS IN
THE SCHOOL!" she says.

"But not today," we think. "Today it is too hot to speak."
She reads us a story about an Eskimo.
He lives in a house made of snow. This Eskimo.
We dream of playing in the snow. Like an Eskimo.
It's still hot and sticky in our school.
Even in our swimming pool it's not cool.
We are sizzling. We are sizzling and frizzling.
It's so hot.

Next day it's sunny, and very, very hot.
Miss Baker tells us, "Tomorrow we're going to the beach.
We'll swim in the sea.

And after that we'll have a picnic tea."
"A picnic tea?" we yell. "Yippee!"
We like the sea better than school.

Next morning Peter Purley is waiting at the gate when we arrive of course. (Peter Purley's always early!)

Our teacher, Miss Baker, brings her guitar.
She sings a song for us and we all join in the chorus –
"Hey! Hey!
Away for the day!
Sunshine and funtime –
A real holiday!" we sing, louder and LOUDER and L O U D E R.
Miss Baker smiles. We all smile. We are the NOISIEST CLASS again!

All our best friends are there.
Peter Purley, always early, Clean Gene, tall and lean,
Mary Bate, always late,
Dirty Bert with his tatty shirt,
Fat Pat, who yowls like a cat,
Steven Fast, always last,

And Hazy Daisy, 'cos she's crazy.
"I'll be first in the water!" yells Dirty Bert, pulling off his tatty shirt.
He has tatty swimming trunks too.

"This time I won't be last," says Steven Fast, dashing down to the sea.
We race across the sands, happy and free!

The waves splash and the sea is blue.
Hazy Daisy asks "What shall I do? Miss Baker! I've forgotten my swimsuit!"
Miss Baker laughs. She knows Hazy Daisy well!
Miss Baker has brought some extra swimsuits with her.
She has been Daisy's teacher for a whole year!
Peter Purley sniffs the air. "Hey! What's that smell?!"
"You!" laughs Hazy Daisy.
"That smell is the smell of the sea," Miss Baker tells us.
"I smelled the smell of the sea before you did!"
Said Peter Purley. "I got to the water early!"
"The sea smells so fresh and clean," smiles Gene.

Steven blows up a rubber ball,
Bigger and BIGGER and B I G G E R.
We all hope it will burst.
But it doesn't.

We splash in the sea.
We hunt for fish.
We hunt for shells.

"I've caught something!" yells Pat.
Pat's caught some seaweed.
"I've caught something!!" cries Mary.
Mary's caught a starfish.
"I've caught something!" calls Bert, looking in the water.
He's caught Steven's feet!
"Hey!" shouts Steven.

"Let's have a swimming race!" cries Mary Bate.
Today she's NOT late! She wins the race. Comes in first place.
Peter Purley comes next,
Clean Gene, tall and lean,

Dirty Bert, WITHOUT his tatty shirt,
Fat Pat, yowls like a cat,
Steven Fast, always last,
And Hazy Daisy, 'cos she's crazy.

"I'm hungry," says Fat Pat. He's brought a lot to eat –
Biscuits and sandwiches and crisps and jelly.
We giggle and laugh at Pat's picnic.
No wonder he's fat!
Pat yells, "There's sand in my sandwiches!"
"That's why they're called SANDWICHES!" we shout.

A man with a red nose and big feet comes by.
He beats very hard on a very loud gong.
"Now listen to me all you bad girls and boys,
I'm going to sing you a song!"
We all groan loudly.
The man with the red nose has a squeaky voice,
like our school bus changing gear.

His song is really funny, we all give him a cheer.
Miss Baker says we should sing our song to him.

It's very noisy, because
Mary Bate is always late,
Peter Purley comes in early,
Dirty Bert and Clean Gene
Cannot sing in tune,
Steven Fast is always last,
And Hazy Daisy doesn't know the words, ('cos she's crazy.)
We are the NOISIEST CLASS ON THE BEACH.
Miss Baker strums her guitar,

11

We all join in the chorus again.
"Hey! Hey!
Away for the day!
Sunshine and funtime –
A real holiday!"
The man with the red nose claps his hands
And beats his gong very loud.

A donkey trots across the sands.
His owner rings a bell. "Donkey rides on Neddy!
Are you ready?" he calls.
But Neddy won't move.
We push and we pull

But the donkey stands still.
"Come on! Let's all push!" cries Peter.
We're all pushing –
  Peter climbs on the donkey's back.
    "Come on Neddy! I'm ready!" he calls.

Neddy runs off at a gallop. Peter holds on! "Good old Neddy!"
Then we all have rides in turn.
Miss Baker waves at us and laughs.
She takes a photo of the NOISIEST CLASS IN THE SCHOOL.

It's the end of the day. Time to go home.
Pick up the spades. Pick up the buckets.
Wave goodbye to the sea.
It's been a lovely day.
The bus is very hot. The seats are soft. We are tired.

When the bus gets back we are all asleep.
"Wake up! Wake up!" calls Miss Baker.
We yawn and stretch our legs.

We are all awake except one.
We say goodbye and thank you to Miss Baker.

The bus is empty except for one.
Can you guess who's still asleep?
It's Steven Fast,
He's ALWAYS last!